THE VELVETEEN RABBIT

A Grosset & Dunlap **ALL ABOARD BOOK**™

TH

VELVETEEN RABBIT

or

How Toys Become Real

By Margery Williams

Illustrated by Florence Graham

Abridged from the original.

Grosset & Dunlap, Publishers

1994 Printing

There was once a velveteen rabbit. He was fat and bunchy, his coat was spotted brown and white, and his ears were lined with pink sateen. On Christmas morning, when he sat wedged in the top of the Boy's stocking, with a sprig of holly between his paws, the effect was charming.

For at least two hours the Boy loved him, and then, in the excitement of looking at all the new presents the Velveteen Rabbit was forgotten.

For a long time he lived in the nursery. He was naturally shy, and some of the more expensive toys snubbed him.

The mechanical toys were very superior, and pretended they were real. The model boat caught the tone and referred to his rigging in technical terms. Even the jointed wooden lion put on airs. The only person who was kind to him at all was the Skin Horse, who had lived longer in the nursery than any of the others.

"What is REAL?" the Rabbit asked the Skin Horse one day. "Does it mean having things that buzz inside you and a stick-out handle?"

"Real isn't how you are made," said the Skin Horse. "It's a thing that happens to you. When a child loves you for a long, long time, you become Real. Generally, by the time you are Real, most of your hair has been loved off, and you get very shabby."

"I suppose you are Real?" said the Rabbit.

"The Boy's uncle made me Real many years ago," said the Skin Horse. "Once you are Real, it lasts for always."

The Rabbit sighed. He thought it would be a long time before this magic called Real happened to him.

One evening, when the Boy was going to bed, he couldn't find the china dog that always slept with him.

"Here," said Nana, who ruled the nursery. "Take your old Bunny. He'll do to sleep with you!"

That night, and for many nights after, the Velveteen Rabbit slept in the Boy's bed.

The Rabbit grew to like it, for the Boy made nice tunnels for him under the bedclothes that he said were like the burrows the real rabbits lived in. And when the Boy dropped off to sleep, the Rabbit would snuggle down under the Boy's warm chin and dream.

The little Rabbit was so happy that he never noticed how his beautiful velveteen fur was getting shabbier, and his tail coming unsewn, and all the pink rubbed off his nose where the Boy had kissed him.

Spring came, and the Rabbit had rides in the wheelbarrow...

and picnics on the grass...

and fairy huts built for him under the raspberry canes.

Once, when the Boy was called away suddenly, the Rabbit was left out on the lawn until long after dusk, and Nana had to come and look for him because the Boy couldn't sleep unless he was there.

"Fancy all that fuss for a toy!" said Nana.

The Boy sat up in bed. "He isn't a toy," he said. "He's REAL!"

When the little Rabbit heard that, he was happy, for he knew
that what the Skin Horse had said was true at last.

One summer evening, the Rabbit saw
two strange beings creep out of the
bracken. They were rabbits like himself,
but quite furry. Their seams didn't show
at all, and they changed shape when they
moved.

"Can you hop on your hind legs?"
asked the furry rabbit.

"I don't want to," said the little Rabbit.
The furry rabbit stretched out his neck and looked.
"He hasn't got any hind legs!" he called out. "And he doesn't smell right! He isn't a rabbit at all! He isn't real!"

"I *am* Real!" said the little Rabbit.
"The Boy said so!"

Just then there was the sound of footsteps, and the two strange rabbits disappeared. For a long time the little Rabbit lay very still. Then the Boy came and carried him home.

One day, the Boy was ill. His face grew very flushed, and his little body was so hot that it burned the Rabbit when he held him close. It was a long weary time....

Presently the fever turned, and the Boy got better. The doctor ordered that all the books and toys that the Boy had played with in bed must be burned.

And so the little Rabbit was carried out to the garden. Nearby he could see the raspberry canes, in whose shadow he had played with the Boy, and a great sadness came over him. Of what use was it to be loved and become Real if it all ended like this? And a tear, a real tear, trickled down his shabby velvet nose and fell to the ground.

And then a strange thing happened. For where the tear had fallen
a flower grew. And out of it there stepped a fairy. She kissed the
little Rabbit on his nose.

"I am the nursery magic Fairy," she said. "I take care of all the playthings that the children have loved. When they are old and worn out and the children don't need them anymore, I come and take them away with me and turn them into Real."

"Wasn't I Real before?" asked the little Rabbit.

"You were Real to the boy," the Fairy said, "because he loved you. Now you shall be Real to everyone."

And she held the little Rabbit close in her arms and flew him into the wood.

In the open glade the wild rabbits danced with their shadows.

The Fairy kissed the little Rabbit again and put him down on the grass.

"Run and play, little Rabbit!" she said.

But the little Rabbit sat quite still.

He did not know that when the Fairy kissed him that last time she had changed him altogether.

He might have sat there a long time if just then something hadn't tickled his nose, and he lifted his hind leg to scratch it.

And he found that he actually had hind legs! Instead of dingy velveteen he had brown fur, soft and shiny, and his ears twitched by themselves.

He gave one leap and the joy of using those hind legs was so great he went springing about...

jumping sideways and whirling round as the others did...

and he grew so excited that when he did stop to look for the Fairy she had gone.

He was a Real Rabbit at last, at home with the other rabbits.

Autumn passed and winter, and in the spring the Boy went out to play in the wood. While he was playing, two rabbits crept out from the bracken and peeped at him.

One of them was golden brown all over, but the other had strange markings under his fur, as though long ago he had been spotted. And about his little soft nose and round black eyes there was something familiar, so that the Boy thought to himself:

"Why, he looks just like my old Bunny that was lost when I had scarlet fever!"

But he never knew that it really was his own Bunny, come back to look at the child who had first helped him to be Real.